This igloo book belongs to:

varalika

Contents

igloobooks

Published in 2015
by Igloo Books Ltd
Cottage Farm
Sywell
NN6 0BJ
www.igloobooks.com

LEO002 1214
2 4 6 8 10 9 7 5 3 1
ISBN: 978-1-78440-178-8

Illustrated by Amanda Enright

Printed and manufactured in China

Fairy Stories

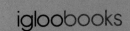

igloobooks

Twinkle's Special Talent

There was going to be a talent show in Fairy Land and all the fairies were very excited. All except Twinkle. "I'm not good at anything," she thought, sadly. "All I can do is fly and any fairy can do that. I wish I had a special talent."

Twinkle took her mind off the talent show by fluttering among the flowers, swooping up high and diving down low. She twizzled and twirled and giggled as she went. She didn't notice her friend, Fenella, watching her. "Go, Twinkle!" cried Fenella, as she watched.

Twinkle was so surprised to hear Fenella's voice that she lost her concentration and her wings froze in mid-air. She tumbled to the ground, landing splat, in a very muddy puddle.

"Oh, dear," she said. "I don't have a special talent and now I can't even fly properly."

"Yes you can," said Fenella excitedly, helping Twinkle out of the puddle.

"You can do loop-the-loops and your dives are brilliant!" cried Fenella. "They're perfect for the talent show."
"I suppose it might be fun to show one or two special moves," thought Twinkle.
"It's time to stop hiding your talent," said Fenella and she jumped off the toadstool and fluttered away.

Twinkle decided to practise her flying moves. She flew up
and down and round and round. She was just about to take a big
dive when she began worrying about the talent show. Suddenly,
Twinkle realized she was falling, down, down, straight into a
sticky spider's web.

Picking off the sticky web silk , Twinkle grumbled and flew up again. She spun round in circles, then imagined flying in front of the talent show judges and making a mistake. Suddenly, Twinkle lost her concentration and before she knew it, she had fallen, thump, onto an open flower.

Just then, the fairy bells rang to announce the start of the talent contest. "I've just got to try my best and not think about falling," said Twinkle, fluttering off. Soon, it was her turn to perform. Swooping into the air to do her first loop-the-loop, Twinkle felt so nervous that her wings wobbled and tipped. She was about to fall when she heard Fenella call to her, "You can do it, Twinkle!"

Suddenly, Twinkle spiralled and soared. She dipped and dived and looped-the-loop so amazingly that the crowd roared and the Fairy Queen awarded Twinkle a gold medal! "I have got a special talent after all," said Twinkle. Now, she was the happiest fairy in Fairy Land.

The Wrong Wand

It was a big day for Fairy Lola. She was going to get her first wand from Fairy Wanda's wand store. Even though Lola got there early, there was already a big queue. There were lots of other fairies who were getting their new wands, too.

As she waited, Lola imagined what her new wand would look like. "I bet it will be pink and sparkly with swirls and a bow tied round it," she thought. However, when Lola finally got to the front of the queue, there was only one wand left.

Wanda gave Lola a wand that looked like a piece of bumpy, old wood. "It may not look pretty," said Wanda, "but this wand is special. You have to figure out how to use it properly."

Lola left the store with her new wand, but she didn't like it at all and she didn't think it was special.

Lola pointed her new wand at a toadstool nearby.
"Alcazo, make it grow," she said, but nothing happened.
Behind her, however, another toadstool grew so large, the little
elf on top almost fell off.
"Wait, little fairy," he said, but Lola just fluttered away.

Lola decided to try her wand on some yellow flowers.
"Alcazink, make it shrink," she said. The flowers in front of Lola
stayed the same, but a flower behind her suddenly shrank, almost
trapping a bee in its petals.
"Stop!" cried the elf and the bee, but Lola didn't hear.

"This wand is rubbish," complained Lola. "If I could find the tree it came from, I would turn it into pumpkins!" she cried. The trees nearby stayed the same but, with a zap and a flash, the one behind Lola turned into two pumpkins.

The elf and the bee finally caught up with Lola.
"LITTLE FAIRY, PLEASE STOP!" shouted the elf.
He told Lola about the giant toadstool, the tiny flower and
the disappearing tree. "They were behind you," he explained.
"Because your wand was pointing in the wrong direction."

"Silly me," Lola said, giggling. She turned her wand around and gave it a swish. A magnificent picnic appeared with cupcakes, strawberries and fruit for them all to share. "I think this is the right wand for me after all," said Fairy Lola and her new friends all agreed.

Cara the Ballerina

There was a buzz of excitement at Miss Primm's ballet school. It was the day before the annual ballet show and the girls were having a final rehearsal. The music played as they lifted their arms and pointed their toes. "That's it, girls," called Miss Primm above the music. "Stretch those arms."

Backstage, Cara followed the movements of the lead ballerina, Isabelle and the other dancers. Cara loved to dance, but she was so shy, she always stayed behind the scenes and painted the props, out of sight. More than anything, Cara wished she had the confidence to dance in the show, just like a real ballerina.

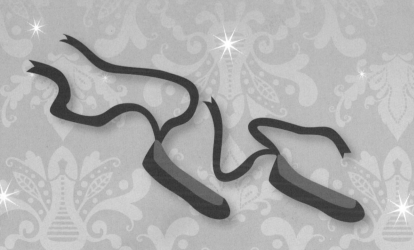

Cara didn't know that Miss Primm had been watching her dance practice. "You are very talented, Cara," she said. "You can do all of the steps and you know Isabelle's routine off by heart. Just believe in yourself and sooner than you think, you will be a proper ballerina."

Cara thought about what Miss Primm had said. That night, as she drifted off to sleep, she made a special wish to be a real ballerina. Soon, Cara had a wonderful dream that she was the star of the ballet, dancing in a sparkling dress in front of a huge audience that clapped and cheered.

When Cara arrived at the ballet school the next day, she could immediately tell something was wrong. Isabelle had tummy ache and didn't feel well at all. "I don't think I will be able to dance in the show," said Isabelle. "I'm sorry, Miss Primm. I wish I had a replacement."

"You do have a replacement," said Miss Primm, pointing at Cara. Everyone gasped, but they knew it made sense. "Of course," said Isabelle, "you know all the steps, Cara, I've seen you practising!"

Cara was really worried, but everyone encouraged her. "Time to get changed," said Miss Primm. "Your wish is about to come true."

Cara changed into a beautiful, pink, sparkly tutu and special ballet shoes. The music began to play and the lights went down. The show was about to begin. "Believe in yourself and magic really can happen," whispered Miss Primm, as Cara took a big, deep breath and stepped onto the stage.

"It's just like my dream," thought Cara, as she whirled and twirled around. Her sequinned tutu glinted in the stage lights, as she stretched her arms and leapt across the stage. The audience clapped and cheered. "My wish came true," said Cara, feeling happier than she could ever remember. "I am Cara the ballerina."

The Rainbow Fairy

Roxy had been given the job of creating beautiful rainbows by the Fairy Queen. The problem was, Roxy didn't know how. She tried flicking her wand back and forth, but just made a few sparkles and a strange grey fog. "Oh, no," said the worried fairy. "What am I going to do?"

Roxy decided to cast a spell. "Green swirl and yellow glow, turn into a bright rainbow," she chanted. Nothing happened, so Roxy sprinkled some fairy dust around. "Atchoo!" The dust got up Roxy's nose and made her sneeze. What would the Fairy Queen say when she heard that the new rainbow fairy couldn't make rainbows?

Roxy flew off into the wood and came across Flutterwing, the wind fairy. "Please help me," said Roxy. "I want to make a rainbow and I don't know how."

"First you need a gust of wind," said Flutterwing, waggling her wand. Suddenly, the wind began to blow. "Now go and find Droplet, the rain fairy."

Roxy found Droplet dipping her toes in the cool water of the waterfall where she lived. "Can you help me to make a rainbow please?" Roxy asked.

"Of course I can," Droplet laughed. She waved her wand and glittering raindrops fell from the clouds. "Now go and see Sunbeam the sun fairy," Droplet told her.

Roxy found Sunbeam watering her flowers. As the two fairies stood on the hill, Sunbeam waved her wand and golden sunlight beamed down, making the raindrops sparkle and shine. "To make a rainbow you need the wind to bring some rain clouds," Sunbeam explained. "Then you add some rain, sunshine and a little magic."

"Your turn, Roxy," said Sunbeam and Roxy waved her wand.
There was a flash of magic and a rainbow rose from behind
the hills.

"What I needed most were my friends," said Roxy, happily.
"It takes teamwork to make a rainbow." Roxy had a brilliant job
and she also had three fantastic friends to share it with.

The Wishing Ring

Katie was playing dress-up in the attic of her gran's house. Katie loved her gran because she always made playtime magical. "How do I look?" asked Katie, showing off her sparkly blue dress and fancy hat.

"You look wonderful," said Gran, giggling and putting on a feather headband.

Gran rummaged around in the dress-up box. "Now let's see what else is in here," she said. Katie saw something glinting in the bottom of the trunk.

"What's that?" asked Katie. Gran reached in and grabbed the object.

"It's what I've been looking for," she said with a smile.

Gran showed Katie a lovely, gold ring with a big, pink stone.
"This is a magical wishing ring," she said. "I'll show you how
it works." Gran put the ring on her finger, twisted it three
times and tapped it. "I wish I had long, purple hair," she said.
Suddenly, Gran's hair began to grow.

It grew longer and longer and turned a sparkly purple.
"Wow, that's amazing!" cried Katie. "I wish my toys would come
to life." She turned and tapped the ring, just like Grandma had.
"That's a good one," Grandma said. "Let's see if it worked."

Katie and Grandma went down the attic stairs and opened
the door to Katie's bedroom. Inside, the toys had come to life!
Dolls were dancing, teddies were twisting around. A flock of fairy
dolls flew past and Katie's rocking horse jumped off his rockers
and trotted over, neighing happily.

"Wow," said Katie. "This is amazing!" She began to dance around like the toys and so did Gran, too. All afternoon, they had fun laughing and playing. "Thank you for finding the wishing ring, Gran," said Katie. "I can't wait to have more magical fun tomorrow!"

The Spooky Shipwreck

Coral, Marina and Shelly loved their home under the sea, but they were feeling bored of always doing the same old thing. They didn't want to sit on rocks or play hide-and-seek in the sea grass. They didn't want to make shell necklaces, either. The mermaids wanted to do something different.

"I know," said Marina, flicking her pink tail and pointing. "Let's go and explore that old shipwreck." Coral and Shelly looked at the ragged sails rippling in the water. They thought the old shipwreck looked really spooky. "It'll be an adventure," said Marina. "Come on, let's go."

The three friends giggled with excitement as they swam across the seabed to the shipwreck. "Look," said Coral, as they all swam a bit closer. "There's a strange light shining below the deck. Let's go and see what it is."

Coral went first and Marina and Shelly followed, through a doorway, inside the shipwreck.

Stairs led down to a corridor with portholes. The mermaids swam along nervously until they came to two other doorways. Suddenly, the ship tilted and creaked. A barrel rolled towards Coral and Shelly caught some clanking chains. "That was close!" they cried, swimming further into the ship.

Just then, they saw the strange light glowing. "It's coming from the ship's ballroom," said Coral and Marina. They swam into the gloomy room where seaweed grew and fish swam. At the end of the room was an old, wooden chest that glimmered and glowed.

Shelly opened the lid and the three friends gasped.
The chest was full of sparkling jewels and coins. "It's a real
treasure chest!" they all shouted together.
"We should tell everyone," Shelly suggested. "If we clean up
this ballroom, we could even have a big party."

The three friends cleaned the ballroom until it looked like new. Then, they invited their mermaid friends to come and have a party. Coral gave each guest a piece of treasure to wear and danced to the music of the best mermaid band, The Fishtails.

"I can't believe we used to think it was spooky in here," said Shelly, looking around at the ballroom full of their friends laughing and chattering. "It's the perfect place for a party."

Everyone had a wonderful time and the three mermaids knew that they would never, ever be bored again.